I HAVE TO START AT SCHOOL TODAY

For everyone starting school –
students *and* teachers – SP

For Ann – GA

SIMON & SCHUSTER

First published in Great Britain in 2020 by Simon & Schuster UK Ltd • 1st Floor, 222 Gray's Inn Road,
London, WC1X 8HB • A CBS Company • Text copyright © 2020 Simon Philip • Illustrations copyright
© 2020 Ged Adamson • The right of Simon Philip and Ged Adamson to be identified as the author
and illustrator of this work has been asserted by them in accordance with the Copyright, Designs and
Patents Act, 1988 • All rights reserved, including the right of reproduction in whole or in part in any
form • A CIP catalogue record for this book is available from the British Library upon request.
978-1-4711-6464-4 (HB) • 978-1-4711-6465-1 (PB) • 978-1-4711-6466-8 (eBook)
Printed in China • 10 9 8 7 6 5 4 3 2 1

I HAVE TO START AT SCHOOL TODAY

Simon Philip and Ged Adamson

SIMON & SCHUSTER

London New York Sydney Toronto New Delhi

I have to start at school today.
"You'll have such fun!" my parents say.

I know they think I'll be OK,

But what if things don't go my way?

I do not feel at all prepared.
My brother said I **should** be scared,

And that was when my
mummy glared.

"You should **not** worry,"
she declared.

And though I know I should ignore
My brother, who's been wrong before,
I'd rather stay in bed for sure,

As I don't know what
lies in store.

Like, what if I can't find the gate?

Or when I do, I see I'm late . . .

. . . And there's a massively irate
Rhinoceros who makes me wait?

I ask, but he won't let me through.
There quickly forms a lengthy queue.
He says that there's a password, too.

I haven't got the faintest clue.

My mum said school will be all right,
That I should not be filled with fright.

The chance these things
will happen's slight.

My brother said
he thinks they might.

... is a selfish bear
Whose bottom leaves no room to share?

And what if he just doesn't care
That I am late and in despair,
And all he does is sit and stare,

Which leaves me pulling
out my hair?

Although Mum said it won't come true,
My brother said it's going to.
It happened to someone he knew . . .

The bear stole her packed lunches, too.

And what if that bear
makes a scene,

Not queuing in
the school canteen,

Then scoffing all
the best cuisine,

Which leaves me with
just one sardine?

"The odds are slim," my mum explained.
"The lunchtime staff are highly trained."

My brother laughed. "When I complained,
The staff just shrugged. The bear remained."

My grandma heard my heavy sighs
And then she took me by surprise.

She shook her head and rolled her eyes.
"Your brother's telling silly lies."

She sat me down upon her knee
And listened very carefully
So I could try to help her see,
How scary school can seem to me.

I said, "But what if through the day
There's nobody who wants to play
And no one even looks my way,
Or checks to see if I'm OK?

Not even when a weird baboon
Arrives to play his loud bassoon,
Performing one, annoying tune

That drives me **mad** all afternoon?"

My Grandma wiped away my tear,
and said she understood the fear,

"You'll be just fine, I promise, dear.
School's better than it might appear."

And then she squeezed me really tight,
And said with kind eyes shining bright,

"There's really no need for your fright.
Just think – what if it all goes **right**?

Like, what if you locate the gate
And find the rhino's **really great**.
He never, ever gets irate
And always helps you
if you're late?

What if you find the selfish bear
Knows stealing's wrong, is quick to share,

And just to show he's full of care
He's used his bum to warm your chair?

The nice baboon won't drive you mad,
Because his music's never bad.

He cheers you up if you are sad –
The kindest friend you've ever had."

My grandma's always very wise
And by my side to sympathise,
And talking made me realise
That school could be a nice surprise.

And after that I saw that I
Should probably give school a try . . .

And once I had, I wondered why
The thought of school had made me cry.

The bear is kind (and warms my seat),
The rhino's helpful, calm and sweet,

Baboon the BEST friend you could meet,
And lunchtime meals are quite a treat!

And now I know what lies in store,
My brother fibbed, of that I'm sure.

My mum and dad were right before.
School's FUN – not scary, any more!